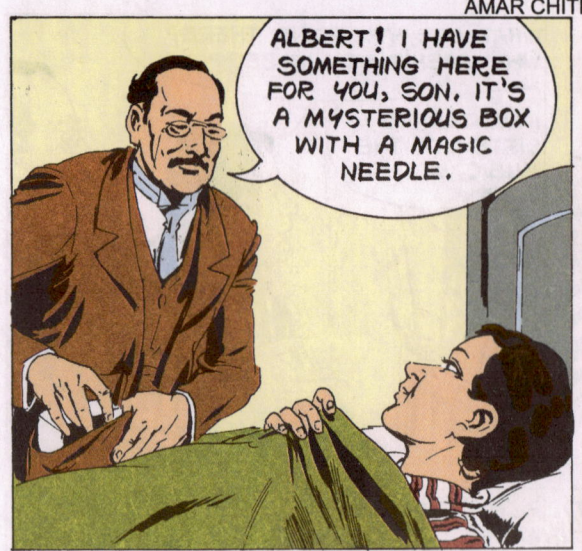

*HERMANN'S YOUNGER BROTHER

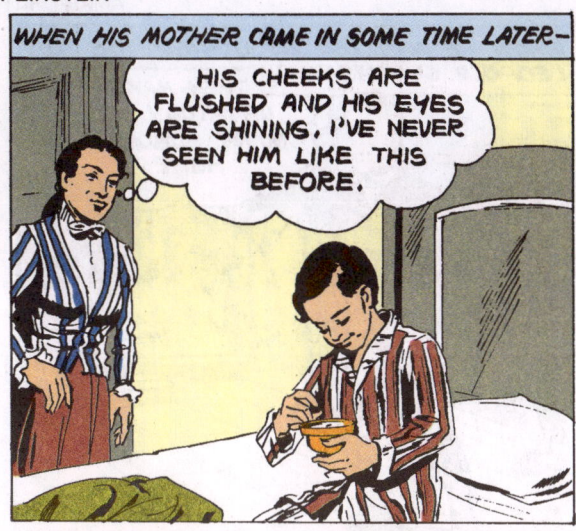

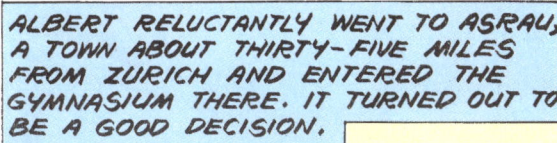

*A PRESTIGIOUS RESEARCH JOURNAL

HE SUBSEQUENTLY SERVED AS A PROFESSOR AT THE UNIVERSITY OF PRAGUE AND THEN AT HIS ALMA MATER, THE SWISS FEDERAL POLYTECHNIC SCHOOL. HE CHANGED JOBS IN EACH CASE EITHER IN THE HOPE OF GETTING MORE TIME FOR HIS RESEARCH OR TO PLEASE MILEVA.

THEN IN 1914 —

MILEVA, I HAVE BEEN OFFERED A MEMBERSHIP BY THE PRUSSIAN ACADEMY OF SCIENCE AT BERLIN.

AS A MEMBER OF THE PRUSSIAN ACADEMY I'LL BE FREE TO DEVOTE ALL MY TIME TO RESEARCH.

YOU AND YOUR RESEARCH! I'VE HAD ENOUGH! YOU CAN GO WHEREVER YOU WANT TO, BUT I'M NOT LEAVING ZURICH!

SO A SAD EINSTEIN HAD TO GO TO BERLIN ALONE.

MILEVA COULD NOT ADJUST HERSELF TO HER HUSBAND'S TOTAL COMMITMENT TO SCIENCE AND SOME TIME LATER THEY WERE DIVORCED.

ALBERT EINSTEIN

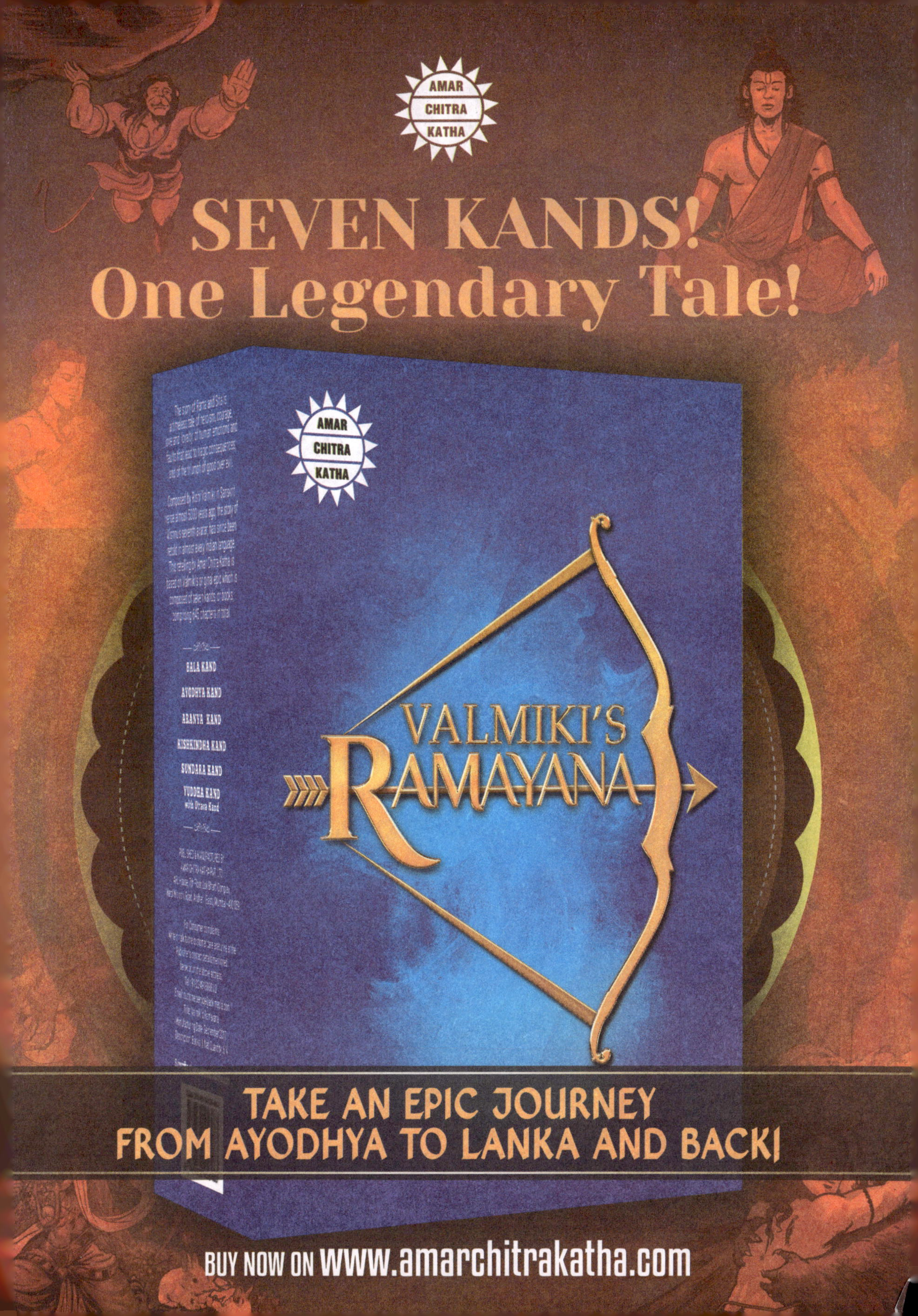

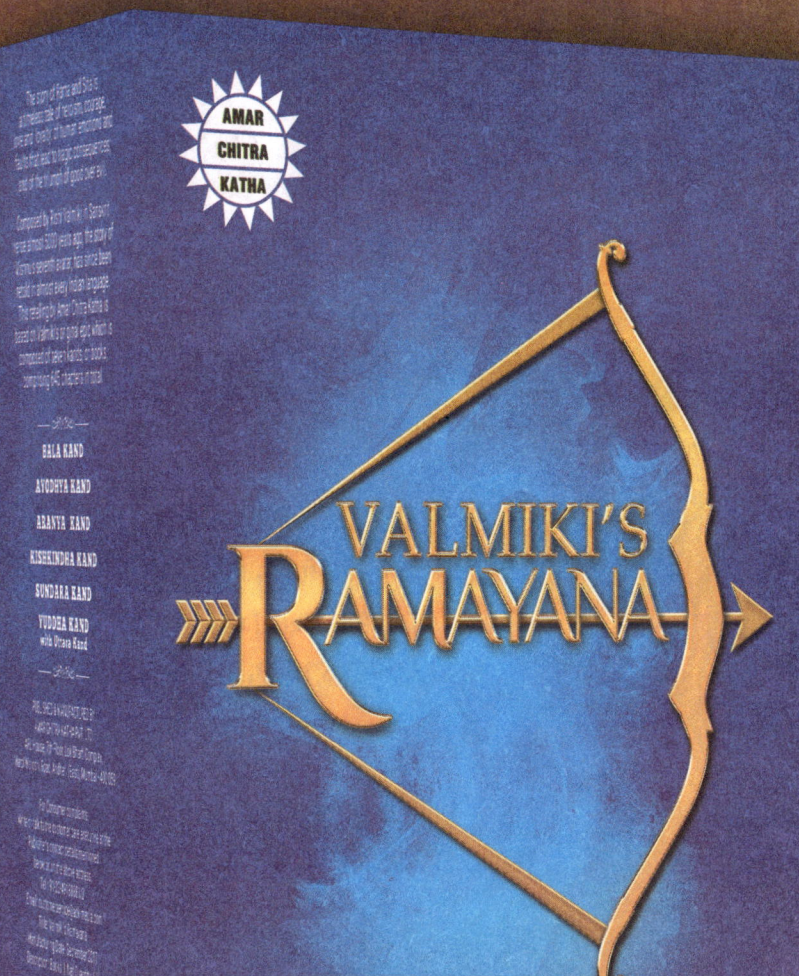

SEVEN KANDS!
One Legendary Tale!

TAKE AN EPIC JOURNEY FROM AYODHYA TO LANKA AND BACK!

BUY NOW ON www.amarchitrakatha.com

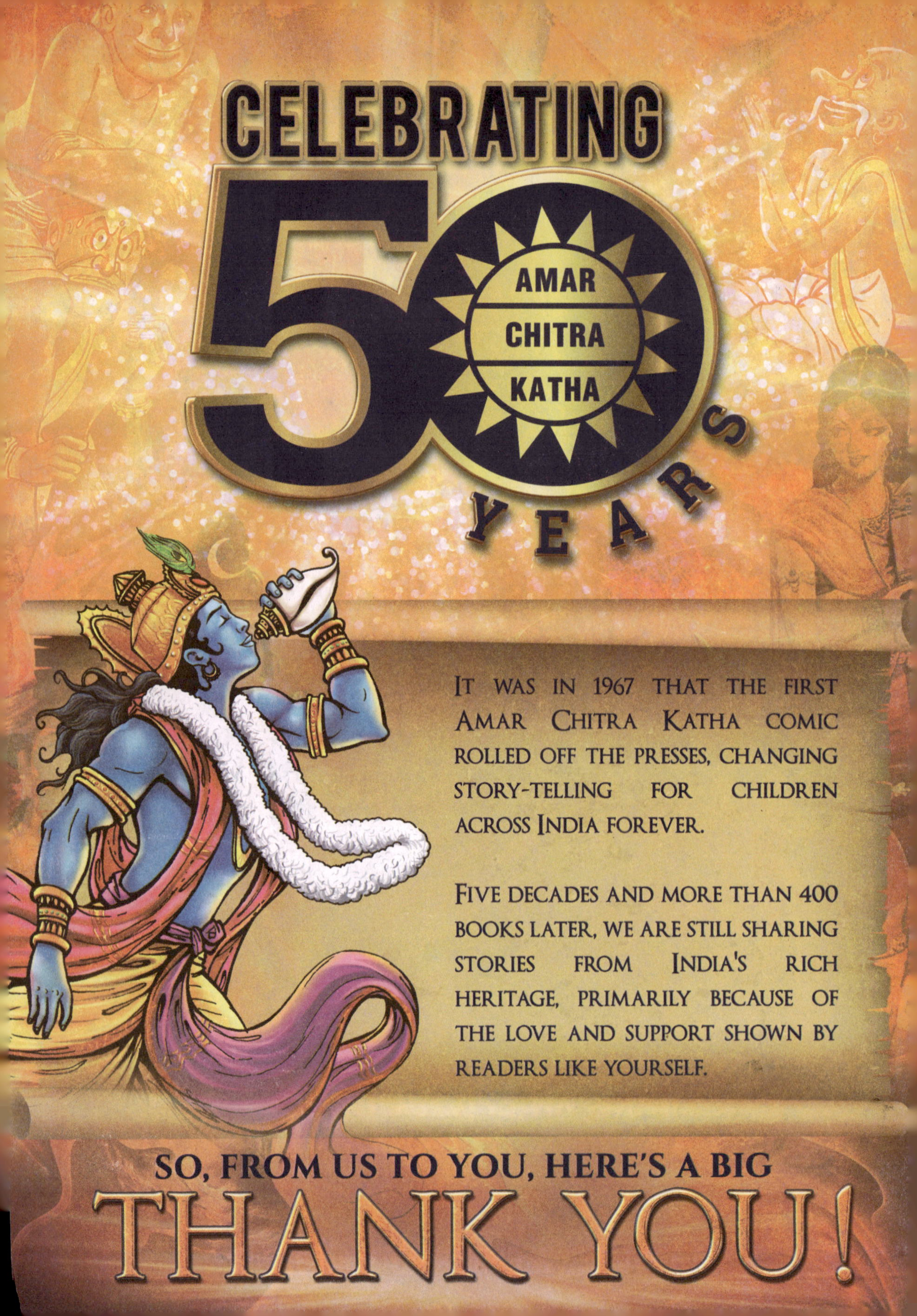

CELEBRATING 50 YEARS
AMAR CHITRA KATHA

It was in 1967 that the first Amar Chitra Katha comic rolled off the presses, changing story-telling for children across India forever.

Five decades and more than 400 books later, we are still sharing stories from India's rich heritage, primarily because of the love and support shown by readers like yourself.

So, from us to you, here's a big

THANK YOU!